Contents

A Play

Car Trouble

Story by Kathryn Sutherland

People in the Play

Narrator

Claire

Lewis

Woman

Miss Greco

Dad

Narrator

The bell rang loudly at the end of the school day.
Children and parents were everywhere.
Cars came and went at the front of the school.

Claire

Dad is late – again!
Everyone else has gone,
but we're still here waiting.

Lewis

He's probably had car trouble.
Let's go back to the classroom
and wait with my teacher.

Claire

No, let's wait here today.
Then we'll be able to see Dad coming.

Lewis

But Miss Greco says we should wait with her
if our parents are late.

Claire

It doesn't matter. Dad won't be long.

We'll stand here by the gate.

Narrator

Minutes later, a blue car came around the corner.

Lewis

That's not Dad.

Claire

No, but it looks like Aunty Jane's car. Maybe she's picking us up.

Lewis

That's not Aunty Jane in the car.

Narrator

The car slowed down. The driver stared at Claire and Lewis. Then, she drove off.

Soon, the same car came past again, and this time it stopped. The driver lowered the window and called to Claire and Lewis.

Woman *(calling)*

Who are you waiting for?

Lewis

Our dad.

Woman

Your dad asked me to pick you up. Get in and I'll drive you home.

Narrator

Claire didn't like the sound of that.
She felt funny inside – uncomfortable.
She knew that her dad would never send a stranger
to pick them up.

Lewis picked up his bag
and walked towards the woman's car.

Claire

No, Lewis! Come back here!

Woman *(to Lewis)*

Come on, love.
You'll come with me, won't you?

Narrator

Lewis wasn't sure what to do.
He just wished that Dad would come.

Lewis looked from the driver to Claire
and back again.
He was about to go to the car
when Claire spoke to the woman.

Claire *(loudly)*

No, thank you.
We'll both wait for our dad.
Come back, Lewis.

Lewis *(in a confused voice)*

But the lady said Dad wants us to go with her.

Claire

I think she's tricking us.
I'm sure Dad will come soon.

Woman *(angrily)*

Your dad asked me to take you home.
Now, get in the car!

Narrator

The children were very frightened,
but Claire knew she had to be brave.
She took a deep breath.

Claire *(loudly)*

No! We will go and wait with our teacher.
Come on, Lewis.

Narrator

Claire grabbed Lewis by the hand
and pulled him towards her.
Then, they ran back to the classroom,
feeling very scared.

Claire *(crying)*

Miss Greco! A lady just tried to make us
get into her car!

Miss Greco

I'm so glad you didn't get into that car.
You were very sensible.

Claire

But we should have come back here,
instead of waiting at the gate by ourselves.

Miss Greco

Yes, but if you can tell me
what the woman looked like,
that will be a big help.
I'll have to ring the police,
because we don't want any other children
getting into that car.

Lewis

She had short brown hair and a red scarf.

Narrator

Then, Claire and Lewis's dad walked into the room.

Dad *(gasping, as if he has been running)*

Sorry I'm late. I had car trouble.

Miss Greco

We've had some car trouble, too.
I was just going to ring the police.

Narrator

Claire and Lewis told Dad all about
the strange woman in the blue car.

Dad

Did you see the number plate?

Claire

No.

Lewis

But the car was just the same as Aunty Jane's car.

Dad

Good. We can tell the police
exactly what it looked like,
and that will help them find the driver.

Claire

It was very hard to say "no" to a grown-up.

Dad

But you trusted your feelings.
You felt that something was wrong, Claire,
and you took care of Lewis.

You both did the right thing,
and I'm very proud of you.

Dad

I'm going to get the car fixed tomorrow, and then I won't be late again.

Lewis

Good.

Claire

Yes. We don't want any more car trouble.

A Play

The Fishing Trip

Story by Mandi Rathbone and Michele Gordon

People in the Play

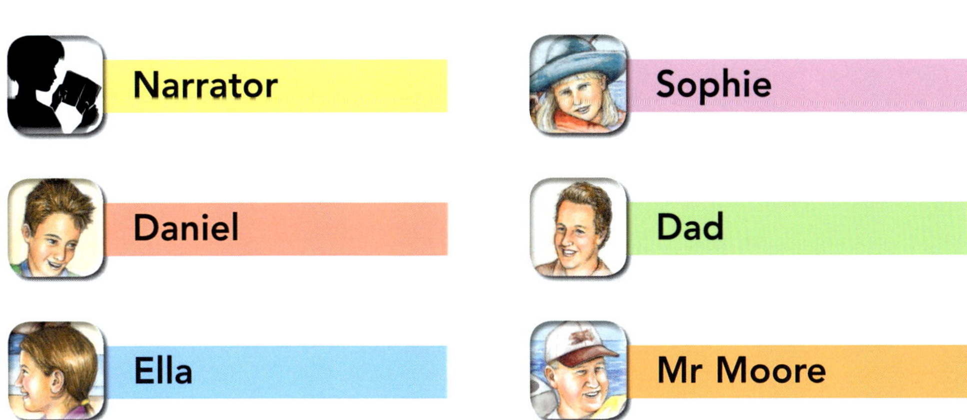

Narrator

Daniel woke up suddenly.
He could hear a noise.
It was his dad talking to him.

Dad

Get dressed quickly, Daniel.
It's a fine day and the tide is right.

Daniel

Great – we're going fishing!

Dad

Hurry up, because Ella's nearly ready.

Narrator

Ella was Daniel's cousin,
and she often stayed for the holidays.
She enjoyed going fishing as much as Daniel did.

Narrator

Daniel walked into the kitchen,
where Ella was eating breakfast.

Ella

Hey, Daniel! I'm going to catch the biggest fish today.

Daniel *(laughing)*

No chance! I'm the fishing champ in this family.

Dad

We're taking two extra people with us today.
They are Mr Moore, who works with me,
and his daughter, Sophie.
Sophie is the same age as you.

Daniel

Oh, Dad! We don't know them.
Do they have to come along?

Dad

It will be fine, Daniel. Sophie has wanted to go on a boat for a long time.

But she's probably going to need some help because she is blind.

Narrator

When they arrived at the boat ramp,
Sophie and her father were waiting for them.

Dad introduced everybody
and handed out the life jackets.

Dad

Now, let's all get into the boat.
Then we can go fishing!

Mr Moore

Come on, Sophie, hold my hand
and climb in over here.

Narrator

Sophie climbed in and felt her way
along the side of the boat towards the seat.
She looked anxious when the boat rocked,
and she almost lost her balance.

As Daniel watched Sophie,
he realised how difficult it must be for her.

Daniel

Don't worry, Sophie.

The boat rocks when we move around.

It will happen again when my dad gets in.

Ella

Here, Sophie. Come and sit by me.
The seat's right beside you.

Sophie *(smiling)*

I can feel the water moving
underneath the boat.
It's exciting!
It feels quite different from being in a car.

Ella

Wait until we get going.
It will be even more exciting then!

Narrator

Daniel's dad took them across the harbour
to his favourite fishing place.

Dad

If you pass me the lines, Daniel,
I'll bait the hooks.

Mr Moore

Here's a rod for you, Sophie.

Narrator

Sophie ran her hands over the rod
and felt the reel.

Mr Moore

You turn the reel to let the line out
or wind it back in again.

Narrator

One by one, they dropped their lines
into the water, and waited for the fish to bite.

Time went by very slowly.
Nobody was getting even a nibble.

Daniel

This is a bit boring.
Can we try another place, Dad?

Ella *(excitedly)*

Wait! I've got a fish – at last!

Narrator

But as Ella wound her line in, the fish slipped off the hook.

Ella *(groaning)*

Oh, no! It got away!

Daniel *(excitedly)*

I've got one now!

Dad

Wind it in, Daniel!

Daniel

Oh, no, it's very small.

Ella *(grinning)*

You know what you have to do, Daniel.

Sophie

What's wrong?

Ella *(giggling)*

Daniel thinks he's the fishing champ,
but he's only caught a little one.

Daniel

And it's too small to keep,
so I'll have to throw it back.

Narrator

They all sat and waited again.

Narrator

After a while, Sophie gave a shout.

Sophie *(excitedly)*

I think a fish is pulling on my line. I can feel it!

Ella

Hold on tightly, Sophie,
because your rod is bending right over.
You must have caught a big one!

Sophie

It must be a big one – it's pulling really hard!

Daniel

Wind some of your line in,
and then let it run back out a little way.
You have to keep doing that.

Mr Moore

You're doing well, Sophie.
Keep winding it in slowly,
and I'll let you know when it's close enough
for me to scoop into the net.

Daniel *(excitedly)*

Here it comes!

Ella

It's a huge one, Sophie,
so you're the fishing champ now!

Narrator

Daniel and Ella felt sorry
that Sophie couldn't see her fish.
Then, they noticed that she was moving her hands
over the fish to get an idea of its size and shape.

Sophie

My fish feels big enough for all of us
to have for dinner tonight.

Thanks for taking me out in your boat.
I've had a great time!